j
S

10,114

Schick, Eleanor
Peggy's new brother

EAU CLAIRE DISTRICT LIBRARY

PEGGY'S
NEW BROTHER

BY ELEANOR SCHICK

PEGGY'S NEW BROTHER

THE MACMILLAN COMPANY, New York, New York

COLLIER-MACMILLAN LTD., LONDON

EAU CLAIRE DISTRICT LIBRARY

77865

Copyright © 1970 Eleanor Schick

Printed in the United States of America
All rights reserved. No part of this book may
be reproduced or transmitted in any form or by
any means, electronic or mechanical, including
photocopying, recording, or by any information
storage and retrieval system, without permission
in writing from the Publisher.

The Macmillan Company
866 Third Avenue, New York, New York 10022
Collier-Macmillan Canada, Ltd., Toronto, Ontario
Library of Congress Catalog Card Number: 70-99124

10 9 8 7 6 5 4 3 2

for Laura and David

Peggy's mother and father had told her
that they were going to have a baby, but
Peggy said she would rather have a dog.

Her mother said that she wasn't old enough
to take care of a dog, and besides, she would
like the baby better, after a while. Peggy began
to wonder if she should have suggested a cat.

Then one morning Peggy's grandmother woke her up and said, "Your father took your mother to the hospital last night. In a few days she'll come home with your baby brother Peter."

When Peter came home, Peggy saw that he
was very small, and he couldn't walk, or talk,
or even sit up. And what was worse, he was
always crying. Everyone was always holding him,
or looking at him, or talking about him. Peggy
was sure that a dog would have been much better.

Peggy wanted to hold the baby herself, and take
care of him, and dress him like she dressed her dolls.
But her mother said that she was still too little,
and she would have to wait until she was a mother.
But they decided, together, that since Peggy was
the big sister now, she could be the helper.

But each time she tried,
everything went wrong.

One time her mother was changing Peter, and Peggy brought the powder, and the diapers and the baby oil.

And in the supermarket, Peggy
tried to reach the jars of baby food.

Even when she tried to stay out
of the way and play by herself,
something would happen.
There was the afternoon
when Peter had just fallen asleep.

Then one day, Peter started crying, and
nothing could make him stop. Peggy's mother
didn't know what to do.

So Peggy decided to help,

and to everyone's surprise, it worked!

After that, whenever Peter was cranky,
Peggy knew how to make him laugh.

She didn't try to wash the dishes.
And she wasn't much help with
preparing bottles, or changing diapers,
but she did have a very special job.

And she decided that she didn't mind
waiting to have a dog. At least until Peter
was a little bigger, and she didn't
have so many important things to do.